THIS **Picture Knight** BOOK
BELONGS TO

....

British Library Cataloguing in Publication Data

A catalogue record for this book is available from the British Library

ISBN 0 340 596236

First published 1991 by Editions Fleurus, Paris, France, as *Kitou Scrogneugneu et Touki Gneugneuscro*
First published in Great Britain 1993

Published by Hodder and Stoughton Children's Books,
a division of Hodder and Stoughton Ltd,
Mill Road, Dunton Green, Sevenoaks, Kent TN13 2YA

Printed in Italy by L.E.G.O., Vicenza

Picture Knight

HODDER AND STOUGHTON

SCRUFFY SCROGGLES
and the Monster Party

by Ann Rocard   Illustrated by F. Ruyer

The character Scruffy Scroggles created by Marino Degano

Once upon a time, there was a horrible, hideous, slobbery little monster with six eyes, called Scruffy Scroggles. He lived in Station Road, Lilyville, in a suitcase under his friend Lucy's bed. No one except Lucy knew he was there, because it was a secret.

Then one day, Lucy went to stay at her grandmother's house.

"Don't be sad, Scruffy," she said. "I'll come home soon."

But Scruffy did feel very sad.

"I'm not going to stay here all on my own for two weeks," he decided. So, when night fell, the little monster opened the window, slid down the drainpipe and jumped into the street.

He walked and walked for hours in the moonlight, along the bank of a wide river and then deep into the forest. In the darkness some of the trees looked a bit like monsters . . .

Suddenly Scruffy came face to face with a bush that looked *exactly* like a monster – in fact it looked just like him! Scruffy went nearer for a closer look. He waggled his ears . . . and the bush did the same!

Scruffy Scroggles burst out laughing.

"Hee-hee-hee!" he chuckled. "I am monstrously stupid! This must be a mirror!"

"Hee-hee-hee!" said the mirror. "I can see my reflection!"

"What?" Scruffy was startled. "A talking mirror?"

Scruffy looked more closely and, in the growing light of dawn, he realised that this was no mirror in front of him – it was a horrible, hideous, slobbery little monster with six eyes, just like him!

Scruffy studied the monster carefully; yes, he was almost an exact double! Only his ears were different: they were green and Scruffy's were blue.

"I must be dreaming!" he exclaimed. "Who are you?"

"Who are *you*?" said the monster.

"My name is Scruffy Scroggles. What's yours?"

"Scroggy Scruffles," the monster replied.

Scruffy was pleased. "I like your name," he said. "It's almost as good as mine. Are you all on your own?"

"Yes," Scroggy answered sadly. "I don't have any friends or anywhere to live."

"No friends!" Scruffy said. "I'll be your friend!"

Scroggy's face broke into a big smile. "Oh great! I was on my way to the Monster Party – will you come with me?"

"That sounds like fun!" said Scruffy. "Yes please!"

So the two little monsters set off hand in hand and soon they found themselves among lots of monsters, all heading for Creepycrawly Castle and the party.

Creepycrawly Castle is where Count Toothsome lives, with his hundreds of pet bats and spiders. Every year, monsters gather at the castle for a Monster Party. They swap their favourite nightmares, boast about the latest tricks they've played, and then they dance rock and roll all night long, beating time on old saucepans.

As they entered the castle, Scroggy told Scruffy that he was hoping the count would give him a job looking after his pets. "Then I'd have somewhere to live," he explained.

But Scruffy was surprised. "Why do you want to do that?" he asked. "Surely you don't like bats and spiders?"

"I love them!" Scroggy answered.

"But you can't like the castle!" said Scruffy.

"I love it!" said Scroggy.

"And what about nightmares?" Scruffy asked.

"Well . . ." Scroggy wasn't too sure.

Just then, Scruffy heard some familiar voices:
Count Toothsome was chatting to four hairy
monsters; four horrible, hideous, slobbery monsters . . .
Did they have six eyes? Scruffy couldn't be sure
because they had their backs to him.

"I thought you had another little rascal with you the last time we met," Count Toothsome was saying.

"Oh, don't talk to us about *him*," growled the father monster.

"That child was such a trial," sighed the mother monster.

"What a blithering blot!" grumbled the grandfather monster.

"My brother was beastly," said the little girl monster, nastily.

Scruffy started to shake. He knew who those monsters were! With his hair standing on end, his knees knocking and his hands trembling, he at last stammered out: "It's my f...f...f..."

"Funnybone?" Scroggy suggested helpfully.

"No, it's my f...f...f..." gasped Scruffy.

"Fleabites?" Scroggy asked, perplexed.

"No, no," Scruffy hissed, "it's my *family*!"

"What! Over there?"

"Yes! They mustn't see me!"

"Why ever not?" asked Scroggy, surprised.

"Because they will want me to go back with them," Scruffy explained in a whisper, "and I don't want to."

How could Scroggy help his friend? Quickly he pushed Scruffy into a corner. "Watch this!" he muttered.

Then he leapt out into the middle of the room and began dancing rock and roll, beating time on an old saucepan like a mad thing and screeching like an owl.

All the monsters clapped as hard as they could and Count Toothsome was astonished.

"Unbelievable!" he cried. "What a fantastic dancer! Who on earth is he?"

"It's Scruffy!" groaned Gruesome Gresham, the father monster.

"My son," moaned Frightful Flavia, the mother monster.

"But Scruffy couldn't dance for toffee," protested Revolting Ronald, the grandfather monster.

"I bet he's still beastly," muttered Nasty Nelly, nastily.

The Scroggles family was baffled. What on earth was he doing there?

Gruesome Gresham strode up to Scroggy. "Scruffy? Don't you recognise me? It's me, your f-"

"Fairy godmother?" Scroggy interrupted quickly.

"Don't be ridiculous!" snapped Frightful Flavia. "It's us, your p-"

"Potatoes?" Scroggy hastily suggested.

"Little monsters were more intelligent in my young day," Revolting Ronald complained crossly. "He needs a good talking to!"

But Scroggy just rolled his eyes and stuck his tongue out.

Nasty Nelly tapped her head and sniggered: "He's completely nuts! Just ignore him!"

But as she turned her back on the little monster, what did she see but another horrible, hideous, slobbery little monster with six eyes, standing in the corner!

"Help!" she screamed. "There's another Scruffy Scroggles!"

Gruesome Gresham and Frightful Flavia were horrified. What could this mean? How many Scruffy Scroggles were there? If there were two here, perhaps there were ten, twenty, *a hundred* roaming round Creepycrawly Castle!

"This isn't fair!" Gruesome Gresham grumbled. "It's just too much!"

"I can't bear it," whimpered Frightful Flavia.

"Little monsters never had doubles in my young day," Revolting Ronald spluttered.

"*Two* beastly brothers?" snarled Nasty Nelly, nastily. "Never! Let's get out of here!" And the whole family ran shrieking from the castle.

Scroggy put down his saucepan and grinned at Scruffy. "Are you happy now?" he asked.

"Yes," Scruffy smiled, "but I don't think Count Toothsome is very pleased with us for frightening his guests away. I think we ought to leave."

"Fine," said Scroggy, and then he whispered, "I don't want to stay here anyway – those bats are very smelly!"

So the two little monsters left Creepycrawly Castle hand in hand.

It was lovely warm weather as Scruffy and Scroggy travelled through the countryside. They leapt over streams, wove flowers into their hair and slept in the sun.

One morning they were doing somersaults in the soft grass, when suddenly Scruffy had a thought.

"Don't you think it's strange that you're my double?" he asked.

"Not really . . ." Scroggy shrugged.

"But where exactly do you come from?" Scruffy wanted to know.

So Scroggy described his funny country. "Beyond the Back-to-Front Mountains is a place called Down-Upside. That's where I come from. Over there, the language is backwards, so a camel is called a melca, and a crocodile is a dileocroc."

"Everyone speaks backwards there," Scroggy continued, "except me." And he hung his head sadly. He had never learnt how to speak backwards and that was why he had had to leave – all the other monsters made fun of him. "I'm hopeless," he sighed.

"You're not hopeless at all!" said Scruffy. "I don't know how to speak backwards either. It really doesn't matter." He thought for a while, then asked, "In backwards language, would a Scruffy Scroggles be a Scroggy Scruffles?"

"Yes," answered Scroggy.

"You wouldn't by any chance have an ancestor who came from my country?" asked Scruffy.

"Yes!" Scroggy replied in amazement. "Scroggy Gruffles, my great-grandfather!"

"Your great-grandfather was called Scroggy Gruffles! Mine was Gruffy Scroggles – they must have been the same monster!" yelled Scruffy. "Yippee! We're cousins!"

Then Scruffy had a brilliant idea. "Why don't you come back to Lilyville with me? I want you to meet my friend Lucy."

So the two little monsters set off for Station Road.

When they arrived, Scroggy felt uneasy. "Won't your friend mind?" he asked nervously.

"Lucy will definitely not mind," said Scruffy. "Don't you worry."

The two cousins quickly climbed up the drainpipe and looked in through the bedroom window. The little girl was unpacking her case. She had just got back from her grandmother's.

Scruffy Scroggles tapped on the window and Lucy ran to open it.

"My Scruffy!" she said. "I've missed you so much!" And she gave him a big hug.

Then she caught sight of Scroggy.

"Oh!" she cried. "I'm seeing double."

Quickly, Scruffy whispered in her ear and Lucy started to laugh.

"You want your cousin Scroggy to live here and be my friend too? Of course he can! It may be a bit of a squeeze, but I think your hiding place is big enough for two."

So these days, in Lilyville, there are two horrible, hideous, slobbery little monsters with six eyes each. Sometimes surprised passers-by may see them waddling across the square, but they usually just rub their eyes and shrug their shoulders and say, "What strange bushes blowing in the wind!"

No, no one knows that Scruffy Scroggles and his cousin Scroggy Scruffles live with their friend Lucy, and no one ever will – it's a secret!

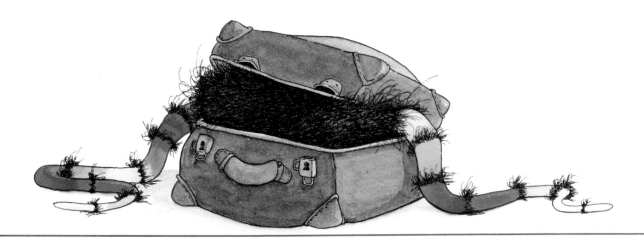